THE GOLDEN BOOK OF
FAIRY
TALES

Illustrated by
WINFIELD HOSKINS

A GOLDEN BOOK • NEW YORK

THE LITTLE GOLDEN BOOKS
ARE PREPARED UNDER THE SUPERVISION OF
MARY REED, Ph.D.
ASSISTANT PROFESSOR OF EDUCATION
TEACHERS COLLEGE, COLUMBIA UNIVERSITY

A COMMEMORATIVE FACSIMILE EDITION PUBLISHED ON THE OCCASION OF
THE 50TH ANNIVERSARY OF LITTLE GOLDEN BOOKS

JACK AND THE BEANSTALK

ONCE UPON A TIME there lived a poor widow with her son Jack.

Jack was a good-natured boy, but too lazy to earn a living. Soon they had nothing left in the world but a leaky hut and an old cow.

"Jack," said his mother one day, "we haven't a

penny for food. You must take the cow to market and sell her."

The sun was warm overhead when Jack started down the road toward town, with the old cow bobbing along behind him.

He hadn't gone far when suddenly, out of a cloud of dust, a strange little man appeared.

"Son," said the little man, "that's a pretty cow. Where are you leading her?"

"To market to sell her," said Jack.

"I'll give you these for your cow," said the man, opening his hand. There in his palm lay the prettiest red and yellow and blue beans that Jack had ever seen.

The more Jack looked at the beans, the more he wanted them.

"It's a bargain," said he, and he took the beans. As the old man led the cow away, Jack patted her for the last time and started for home.

"Mother, see what I got for the cow," he cried as he flung open the door.

"A handful of beans!" she wept angrily. She tossed the beans out of the window. "Now we can have no supper!"

4

It was a hungry Jack who sobbed himself to sleep that night.

But when he awoke the next morning, a strange sight sent him leaping out of bed to the window. Leaves the size of elephants' ears shaded his room!

"That's odd!" he exclaimed. "They weren't here last night!"

He hurried outdoors. There was a tall green beanstalk reaching far, far up in the sky. It had grown from the beans!

"It must have a top," thought Jack, staring upward till his neck was stiff. "I'll climb till I reach it."

And up, up, up the beanstalk he climbed, till the hut below was nothing but a black speck.

At last the beanstalk ended on top of a cloud. Jack saw a tremendous stone castle with high towers and a moat.

He found his way into the castle. After wandering through its echoing halls he entered the great kitchen, where the cook was removing an enormous pan of bread from the oven.

When the kind old cook saw Jack, she dropped the pan with a clatter.

"Don't you know that a vicious Giant owns this castle? He eats boys like you," she warned.

Suddenly the floor shook and the walls trembled.

"Here he comes!" whispered the cook. "Hurry! Hide!"

Just as Jack climbed into the cupboard, a fierce Giant, about four stories high, stamped into the room.

"Fee, fi, fo, fum, I smell the blood of an Englishman," he roared, swinging his club. He sniffed in all the corners; he sniffed under his big chair; and then he sniffed near the cupboard.

" 'Tis nothing but roast pork," quavered the old cook, setting a huge steaming platter on the table.

"Roast pork!" said the Giant. It was his favorite dish! To Jack's relief, he fell to eating at once.

Jack hungrily watched the Giant gobble down enough dinner for twenty.

Then the Giant called for his magic hen. The cook brought it.

"Lay a golden egg," the Giant roared, and in a twinkling, a golden egg shone on the table.

"That's a handy hen to own," thought Jack.

And when at last the Giant's head nodded in a snooze, Jack slipped out of the cupboard, quietly tucked the hen under his arm, and fled down the beanstalk to his home.

In no time the magic hen made Jack and his mother rich.

8

The weeks flew by. Then one summer day Jack decided to climb the beanstalk again. Once more he stole into the Giant's castle.

This time when the Giant's footsteps shook the castle, Jack hid under the table.

The Giant sniffed about in the corners.

"Fee, fi, fo, fum, I smell the blood of an Englishman," he roared.

" 'Tis roast goose," said the cook, and again the Giant sat down to his dinner. He then counted his gold and fell asleep.

While the Giant was napping, Jack ran off with two bags of gold, and arrived home safely.

Win Hoskins

The third time Jack went to the castle, the Giant had his dinner and then called for his magic harp. When he fell asleep, Jack stole out of the cupboard, snatched the harp, and ran for the beanstalk.

But the magic harp began to tinkle a tune. Back in the kitchen the Giant awakened with a grunt that shook the castle.

"Fee, fi, fo, fum, I smell the blood of an Englishman!" he thundered. "And this time I'll catch him!"

He ran out of the castle after Jack.

"Catch me if you can," shouted Jack, reaching the beanstalk.

Then down the beanstalk he hustled, with the Giant close behind him.

Down, down, down he climbed, in the shadow of the Giant. He had to hold on tight; the beanstalk trembled and shook.

And closer and closer and closer came the Giant, till his breath was a powerful wind that almost blew Jack away.

Jack heard his mother scream.

"Mother, Mother," he called, "get me the ax from the shed!"

At last Jack slid to the ground. Snatching the ax from his mother, he chopped the beanstalk through.

Down fell the beanstalk to the earth, and down,

down fell the Giant. He crashed to the ground below, burying himself deep in the earth.

And that was the end of the Giant. But Jack and
his mother, wealthy with the riches Jack had
brought from the castle, lived happily ever after.

CINDERELLA

O<small>NCE</small> <small>THERE</small> <small>WAS</small> a beautiful girl who was kept busy scrubbing and cleaning by an unkind step-mother. The girl was called Cinderella by her two ugly stepsisters, because she was always sprinkled with cinders from the fireplace.

Though there was nothing too fine for her step-sisters to wear, Cinderella was always clad in rags. From dawn till sundown she was busy at home, while her stepsisters spent their time shopping or riding in their coach to show off their finery.

One day the stepsisters were invited to a grand ball to be given by the King's son.

"I shall be beautiful in my red velvet gown," said the elder.

"It's not half so fine as my green one," said the other.

There seemed to be no end to their arguments and their fussing as the day of the ball approached.

Cinderella was kept running from one to the other, with nothing but cross words for her pains.

"Cinderella, press my ruffles," ordered one step-sister.

"After you shorten my sleeves," ordered the other. And poor Cinderella tried to please them both.

At last came the day of the ball. The household hummed with excitement.

As Cinderella dressed the hair of her stepsisters and fastened their jewels into place, they quarrelled with each other as to which looked the prettier.

Then the older sister turned to Cinderella, and tauntingly said:

"Cinderella's dress is the most becoming. Why don't you go to the ball, Cinderella?"

Cinderella looked down at her rags and choked back her tears.

And after her stepsisters had driven off to the ball, she wept alone by the fireside.

"Why are you weeping, Cinderella?" suddenly asked a strange sweet voice.

Looking up, Cinderella saw her Fairy God-mother standing before her. She was the most beau-tiful lady Cinderella had ever seen.

"I wish—I wish I could go to the ball," sobbed Cinderella.

"And so you shall," said her Godmother, wav-ing her wand.

In a flash, Cinderella's rags changed into a daz-zling white gown! On her feet were the daintiest slippers she had ever seen! They were made of glass.

"Bring me a pumpkin," said her Godmother.

A pumpkin seemed a queer thing to take to a ball, but Cinderella hurried to the vegetable patch and brought back the biggest one she could find.

A touch of the wand—and right before Cinder-ella's eyes the pumpkin changed into a golden coach!

"Bring me that cage of mice," said the good Godmother. "Mice can be useful, too."

Cinderella lifted the cage from the corner, and right before her eyes, four of the mice changed into horses, and the fifth and fattest became the coachman. The horses neighed, and the coachman stroked his whiskers.

"Now you may go to the ball," said the Fairy Godmother. And Cinderella had never been happier.

"But be sure to leave by midnight," warned her Godmother, "or you will return in rags." Then the Godmother vanished.

Tears of joy filled Cinderella's eyes as she was driven to the ball in her glittering coach.

When Cinderella entered the grand hall of the palace, a hush fell over the guests.

"Who is the beautiful princess?" they whispered.

The Prince hurried to Cinderella's side, and throughout the evening would dance with no one else.

Cinderella was especially kind to her stepsisters. Never for one moment did they dream that the beautiful princess in the spangled gown was the cinder maid they had left at home.

But in her happiness, Cinderella forgot her Godmother's warning.

Suddenly the clock began to strike.

Dong! Dong! Dong!

It was almost midnight!

Quick as a flash, Cinderella darted from the ballroom, but as she ran, she dropped one of her glass slippers on the steps.

By the time she had reached the gate, all her splendor was gone. She found herself in rags, with a big orange pumpkin and five scurrying mice close by.

The Prince had rushed after Cinderella, but she had been too swift for him. He asked the guard at the gate if he had seen a beautiful Princess.

"Only a scullery maid, Your Highness," said the guard sleepily.

Then the Prince discovered the glass slipper on the steps. It was the tiniest slipper he had ever seen.

Said he, "Whoever can wear this glass slipper shall become my wife."

Day after day, the Prince and his herald searched through the land for its owner. They tried the slipper on hundreds and hundreds of fine ladies.

But some feet were too big, and some too wide,
And none of the feet would fit inside.

At last the Prince and his herald arrived at the home of the stepsisters.

Each of the sisters painfully tried to squeeze a foot into the slipper, but it was many sizes too small.

"Is there anyone else?" asked the Prince, very disappointed.

"Only a cinder maid," they answered laughing. "Don't waste your time."

"Bring her forth," insisted the Prince. And Cinderella was led blushing from behind the kitchen stove.

She put out her little foot as the herald knelt

before her. Her sisters gasped. The slipper slid on with ease!

"A perfect fit!" they exclaimed, hardly believing their eyes.

The Prince was overjoyed. "It is the Princess!" he said.

Then, as Cinderella drew forth the other glass slipper from her apron pocket, her Fairy Godmother appeared. The good fairy waved her wand, and there was Cinderella as the beautiful Princess of the ball!

Cinderella's sisters fell on their knees and begged forgiveness for the way they had treated her. Cinderella was much too kind to bear them any grudge. She invited them to visit her at the palace, for now she was to marry the Prince.

The wedding took place within the week, and Cinderella and the Prince lived happily ever after.

PUSS IN BOOTS

Once there was an old miller who left nothing to his youngest son but a cat.

"What can I do with a cat?" asked the poor fellow. "I shall die of hunger."

The cat heard the words of his master and said, "Give me a pair of boots and a bag, and I will make you rich."

The young man laughed. "How can a cat make me rich?"

But he had so little to lose that in his despair he gave the cat the boots and the bag.

Puss drew his new boots on his feet, and filling the bag with grain, he hung it about his neck. Then off he went to the woods.

Suddenly Puss sniffed a rabbit. He opened the mouth of the bag, and quietly waited in the grass.

Hop, hop, hop went the rabbit, smelling the grain. Hop, hop, hop—right into the open bag. Quick as a flash, Puss pulled the strings with his paws. Then he hung the bag around his neck and hurried to the palace of the King.

Puss bowed low before the King. Pulling out the rabbit by the ears, he said:

"My master sends you this rabbit."

"And who is your master?" asked the King.

"The Marquis of Chizzelwitt," said Puss without a moment's hesitation.

"Send your master my thanks," said the King.

The next day Puss came to the King again.

"My master sends you these pheasants," said he, opening his bag.

"And who is your master?" asked the King.

"The Marquis of Chizzelwitt," answered Puss.

Again and again, Puss trapped some game for the King and presented them in the name of the Marquis.

"The Marquis of Chizzelwitt must be a great hunter," thought the King.

One day the King and his daughter were to drive near the banks of the river. The news reached the ears of the cat.

"This is your chance," said Puss to his master. "Bathe in the river this morning, and I will tend to the rest."

His master consented, and they went down to the river.

No sooner did Puss hear the wheels of the royal coach than he rushed out of the bushes.

"The Marquis of Chizzelwitt is drowning!" he shouted. "Save him!"

The King at once sent his men running to the river, and they dragged Puss's master from the water.

Puss explained to the King that someone had stolen his master's clothes. So the King sent for the finest suit in his palace.

When the suit was brought, Puss's master put it on. Arrayed in his new splendor, he looked so very handsome that he was invited to ride in the King's coach. And sitting beside the King's daughter, in no time at all he won her heart.

Puss ran ahead of the carriage, and to all he met he said:

"Tell the King this land belongs to the Marquis of Chizzelwitt, or you shall be mincemeat by morning."

Then as the King passed and asked of those in the field, "To whom do these lands belong?" the answer was always, "The Marquis of Chizzelwitt, of course."

The King was amazed at the great estates of the
young man.

Puss then led the carriage to the castle of the Ogre to whom those very lands belonged. He ran ahead, and found the Ogre in his great hall.

"I have heard," said Puss, bowing low before him, "that you can change into a lion. I don't believe it."

"I will prove it," said the Ogre, who was a show-off. In a flash, he became a fierce, roaring lion. Puss jumped up on a shelf for safety until the lion changed into the Ogre again.

"I have heard," said Puss after complimenting the Ogre on his performance, "that you can change into a mouse. I don't believe it."

"I will show you," said the Ogre. In a flash, he was scurrying across the floor as a tiny mouse.

And in no time, Puss had pounced upon him— and there wasn't any mouse or Ogre any more!

Then Puss ran to meet the King and his master in the carriage at the gate.

"Welcome to the castle of the Marquis of Chizzelwitt," said Puss, bowing low.

Then they all entered the castle, and found a feast awaiting them in the great hall.

"You are a rich and great man," said the King to Puss's master when the feast was over. "I should be proud to have you as a son-in-law."

Puss's master and the Princess were overjoyed. And the wedding was celebrated that very day.

Then Puss in Boots was made Chief Lord of the Castle and was served mice on a golden platter.

And the Marquis of Chizzelwitt and his beautiful bride lived happily ever after.

THE SLEEPING BEAUTY

Once upon a time a baby princess was born to a King and a Queen. The King and the Queen had asked the five good fairies to the christening, but they had not invited the bad fairy.

The castle was lit with countless candles for the celebration. A grand feast had been prepared and was served to the fairies on golden platters.

As the evening drew to a close, the good fairies clustered around the crib.

They gave the most wonderful gifts to the new Princess—the gift of wit and the gift of beauty, the gift of grace and the gift of joy.

35

When four of the fairies had made their magic wishes beside the little crib, the casement window was flung open.

In flew the bad fairy in her ugly black robes.

She pushed aside the startled good fairies and leaned over the Princess in a temper.

"I have a gift, too," said she with a sneer. "At the age of eighteen, you shall prick your finger on a spindle and die."

"Die at eighteen!" echoed the good fairies, thunderstruck, and the King and the Queen wept.

The fifth fairy stepped forward.

"Do not mourn," said she gently. "I have not yet made my wish. I cannot entirely undo the spell. But the Princess shall not die when she pricks her finger. She shall fall asleep for a hundred years, until the kiss of a prince shall awaken her."

A nap of a hundred years seemed much too long to the King. So the next day he issued a decree that all spindles in the kingdom be burnt at once.

There wasn't a spindle left even in the museums!

The years passed by, and the Princess grew into a young lady. The fame of her wit and beauty, her grace and joy, spread through many lands.

But on her eighteenth birthday, the Princess took a fancy to wander through the castle. In a forgotten room in the highest tower, she came upon an old woman busily turning a spinning wheel.

"What are you doing, good dame?" asked the Princess.

"Spinning, spinning, my pretty one."

"Will you let me try?" asked the Princess.

"Gladly," answered the old woman as she moved aside.

But the Princess was careless. No sooner had she touched the spindle than she pricked her finger and fell to the ground in a deep sleep.

At the same instant, the King fell asleep over his papers, the Queen over her breakfast, the Baker over his pie. Even the mice in the walls fell to dozing, and a deep silence was over all.

For a hundred years, the spell hung over the castle. A high thorny hedge grew up around its borders and hid the highest towers.

Time and again, some prince who had heard the legend of the Sleeping Princess found his way to the castle. Each tried desperately to cut through the wall of thorns, and each gave up in despair.

So the full hundred years passed by.

Then one day a handsome Prince in search of shelter for the night saw the towers of the castle from a mountain top. He rode up to the thorny hedge and touched it with his sword.

To his surprise, it parted before him.

In front of the arched doorway of the castle stood a guard asleep with a spear in his hand.

"To whom does this castle belong?" asked the Prince in a very loud voice.

His only answer was an echo.

There seemed to be no waking the guard, even though the Prince shook him.

The bewilderment of the Prince grew as he wandered through the silent halls of the castle. For there, frozen in the same strange sleep, were the pages and the footmen and the dogs and countless others.

At last the Prince reached the highest tower. There was the Princess asleep where she had fallen.

Her lips were rosy red, and the flush of health was still on her cheeks. She looked so beautiful as she lay there, with her golden hair in waves over the floor, that the Prince bent over and kissed her.

Instantly the Princess awoke, and smiled up at the Prince.

At the same moment, the King sat up to work on his papers; the Queen went on with her breakfast; the Baker put the pie in the oven; the mice scurried out of their holes. The castle stirred with life.

They were all still too sleepy to realize what had happened.

Suddenly the King jumped up.

"The spell is broken," he shouted. "The Prince has come!"

There was a great festival in the castle that night, and the bells rang out through the countryside.

So that very night they were married. And they lived happily ever after.